Rotten Teeth

For Norman, because of your good ideas
—L.S.

To Danny, my little brother
—D.C.

www.houghtonmifflinbooks.com

Library of Congress Cataloging-in-Publication Data
Simms, Laura.
Rotten teeth / written by Laura Simms ; illustrated by David Catrow.
p.   cm.
Summary: When Melissa takes a big glass bottle of authentic pulled
teeth from her father's dental office for a show-and-tell presentation,
she becomes a first-grade celebrity.
RNF ISBN 0-395-82850-3 PAP ISBN 0-618-25078-6
[1. Show-and-tell presentations—Fiction. 2. Schools—Fiction.]
I. Catrow, David, ill. II. Title.
PZ7.S5919Ro 1998
[E]—dc21   97-2528 CIP AC

Manufactured in the United States of America
WOZ 10 9

Rotten Teeth

Laura Simms   Illustrated by David Catrow

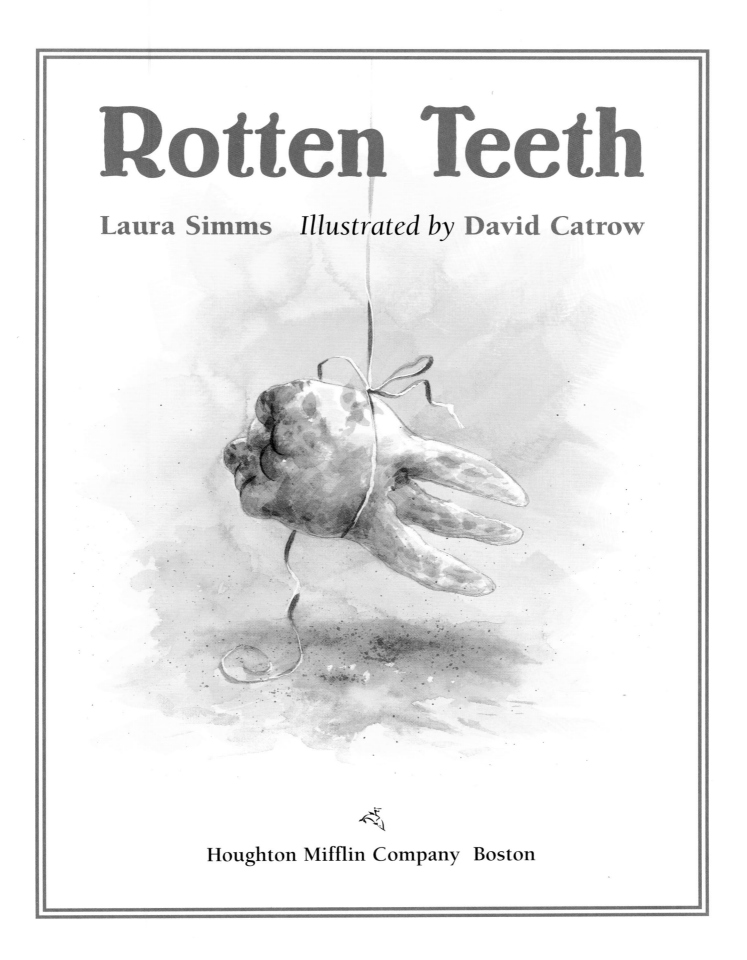

Houghton Mifflin Company Boston

Melissa Hermann was the shortest person in her first-grade class. She was also the only one who hadn't brought in anything for Show and Tell.

Elaine Estes showed the class a plastic dinosaur footprint. Carmine Appaseed shared his entire glow-in-the-dark sticker collection. Even shy Fern Miller had brought in her baby hamster. It sat in a cage in the room all morning.

But nothing from Melissa's house seemed special enough.

She decided it was time to ask her brother for help.

Norman was seven years older than Melissa, and she thought he was very smart. "Norman," she said, "I can't find anything interesting in our house to take to school for Show and Tell—I mean something kids would *like*."

Norman was quiet for a moment. "Let me think about it," he said. "This is important."

Melissa was glad to be understood.

"I know," he said finally. "How about the bottle in dad's dental lab?"

Melissa's eyes grew wide. Her brother was absolutely right. The bottle was the most fascinating thing in their house.

At the back of their father's dental office was a big glass bottle of authentic pulled teeth floating in a funny yellow liquid. The old teeth were all gray and green, with long ugly dangling roots twisted together. "Perfect," said Melissa. "I'll ask Dad."

Norman said, "Dad's busy. I'll help you."

The next morning, Melissa and Norman woke early and washed all the teeth. There were exactly thirty-one.

"Just enough for each first-grader to have their own," Norman pointed out.

So no one could guess what Melissa was bringing to class, they slipped the bottle into a brown paper bag. Norman walked Melissa to the door of her classroom.

"Good morning, Melissa," said Mrs. Swann.

Shyly but proudly, Melissa lifted the brown shopping bag. "I brought something for Show and Tell."

"That's lovely," Mrs. Swann answered, patting Melissa's head.

After attendance and morning lessons, Mrs. Swann announced, "Today, class, Melissa Hermann has something to share for Show and Tell. Let's sit up straight and give her our attention."

Most kids thought Show and Tell was boring. But Melissa Hermann, who was usually quiet, and whose large eyes always seemed to be watching everyone, had never brought in anything before. She had never spoken in the front of the room, and her brown bag looked mysterious. So when she walked to the front of the room, the class grew still.

Melissa was nervous. What if the kids hated the bottle? What if they laughed at her? She shifted from one foot to the other. She wished she had planned what to talk about. She should have asked her brother for advice. She couldn't think of anything to say.

Finally she opened up the bag, held up the bottle, and blurted out,

"ROTTEN TEETH! FROM REAL MOUTHS!"

At once the entire class leaned forward. Melissa shook the bottle so the teeth floated and the roots wiggled.

"Yuck!" cried Fern Miller.

"Are they real?" called out Carmine.

Melissa nodded enthusiastically.

"Weird," shouted Alfonse.

"Was there *blood*?" shrieked Richard Sherman.

One first-grader after another called out questions: "Did you see them being pulled? Was anybody screaming? How old are they?"

Melissa began placing one tooth on top of each child's desk and talking excitedly.

"My father's dental office is in our house. I hear everything. One day I was sitting in the kitchen and I heard the sound of the drill and then I heard a boy screaming, and his mother said—"

Just as Melissa was getting to Elaine Estes's desk, Mrs. Swann swooped out from behind her big desk and cried, "Melissa Hermann, this is *not appropriate.*"

For the first time Melissa understood the words "not appropriate." She could tell by the way Mrs. Swann was lifting up each tooth, holding it far from her face as if it were a little dead rat, and dropping it swiftly into the bottle.

Melissa sat down quietly, and no one in the class said a word.

After collecting all the teeth, Mrs. Swann twisted the lid shut, put the bottle back in the brown paper bag, and hid it under her desk. "Math lesson," she announced. The children opened their notebooks.

Melissa couldn't concentrate. This day, she decided, was the worst day of her life, worse than the day her mother forced her to wear the "sensible" red sweater with two large brown dogs on the front to school. (Her Aunt Zelda had bought it in a thrift shop.) She vowed that she would never bring anything to Show and Tell. She would never say anything in the front of the class again!

But at recess Melissa was popular. The kids gathered around her in the schoolyard to hear more about the teeth. Forgetting her promise not to speak, Melissa told them stories about the dental office, especially about the little dark room at the back where the bottle was stored. Mostly, everyone was interested in the gory details: the moans, the blood on the towels, the size of needles, and the sound of drills.

Melissa got excited. She even told about her Uncle Jack from Texas. "He wore his cowboy hat and boots even while he had his teeth fixed. Once he moaned so loudly in the office that my mother played piano so we wouldn't have to hear it." She described everything in detail, adding new details that she had never thought of before just to make the story better.

That afternoon, at her desk after recess, Melissa imagined more stories. Stories that took place in her living room, her basement, and her attic. Stories about all the special things in her house.

She couldn't wait to tell Norman about her great success as a storyteller.

But at three o'clock Norman was not waiting at school as usual to take her home. Neither was her mother. Her father was. Mrs. Swann had called him during recess.

Over pizza and Cokes at Lenny's Kosher Pizzeria, Melissa promised never to take anything for Show and Tell again without first asking permission.

By the time she finished her second slice of pizza, she had thought of lots of interesting things in the house to take to school. "How about the real bear-claw necklace that Mom keeps in her dresser?" Her father looked a little uncomfortable. Melissa added helpfully, "Or maybe the doll's bed you once made for me from dried orange peels? It still smells."

Dr. Hermann smiled. "I don't think you'll be needing any more good advice from your brother."

Melissa grinned. "Maybe I should take *Norman* in for Show and Tell!"

From that day on, Melissa Hermann loved Show and Tell, especially the tell part. No matter what she took, she always told the most interesting stories.

And at the end of the year, when the class voted on the Absolutely Most Special Show and Tell of the Whole Year, the class agreed: it was Melissa Hermann's ROTTEN TEETH.